THIS WALKER BOOK BELONGS TO:

_____

_____

_____

_____

First published 1986 in Germany by Loewes Verlag as
Wo bliebt der Weihnachtsmann?

Published 1988 exclusively for Mothercare U.K. Ltd
by Walker Books Ltd, 87 Vauxhall Walk,
London SE11 5HJ

This edition published 1991 by Walker Books Ltd

Text © 1986 Norbert Landa
Illustrations © 1986 and 1988 Hanne Türk
English translation © 1988 Patricia Crampton

Printed in Hong Kong by
Sheck Wah Tong Printing Press Ltd

CIP information is available

ISBN 0-7445-2080-0

BRUIN

Where Is Father Christmas?

Written by
Norbert Landa

Illustrated by
Hanne Türk

Translated by
Patricia Crampton

WALKER BOOKS
LONDON

It was five days to Christmas
and all the fields were still green.
There was not a snowflake to be seen anywhere.

Bruin and Susie Bruin had made out their lists
for Father Christmas days ago.
"A big drum for Bruin.
A flute for Susie Bruin and
a mouth-organ for Grandpa Bruin."
Now Bruin added in big, fat letters,
"Important! Snow! Express!
Only four days to Christmas."
Christmas without snow is like
honey without a honey-pot.

Next morning the snow began to
fall in thick, soft flakes.
"Snow, snow!" Susie Bruin cheered.
"More snow, please, because
it's only three days to Christmas!"

One day later there was too much snow for
them to shovel, too much snow to go out
in, too much snow for almost anything.
"Then we'll make everything cosy indoors,
and bake Christmas biscuits,"
said Grandpa Bruin. "The
day after tomorrow
is Christmas Day!"

The next day, when Grandpa Bruin, Susie Bruin
and Bruin looked out of the window, they could
see nothing but snow, snow and more snow.
"We're snowed in!" said Grandpa Bruin.
"If Bruin House can't be seen,
who knows if Father Christmas
will be able to find us tomorrow?"

Christmas without Father Christmas is even
worse than Christmas without snow.
Christmas without Father Christmas
is like a honey-pot without honey.

"*Un*happy Christmas!" said Bruin. "We're snowed in, Father Christmas won't find us, and the poor birds outside won't be able to find any food in the snow and they'll starve!"

"But why should the birds starve?"
said Susie Bruin.
"We've baked so many biscuits,
we can easily give them some!"

"Bup me carmp gim our bifkifs amay!"
said Bruin with his mouth full.

Oh yes, they could.

So the Bruins gave a
Christmas biscuit party
for hungry birds.

"Look, over there!" Susie Bruin said,
pointing excitedly at Bruin House.
"I just saw Father Christmas!"

"Where?" said Bruin. "Where? Where?"

"Let's go and look in the house,"
Grandpa Bruin suggested.

"Father Christmas has been here!"
laughed Susie Bruin. "And I was the one,
I was the one who saw him!"
Then, among the presents, they found this letter.
"Dear Bruins,
I almost didn't find you. Perhaps there really was
a little too much snow. But then I saw a flock of birds
and followed them.
That was how I found
Bruin House!
In haste,
Yours truly,
Father Christmas."

It was the most wonderful Christmas
the Bruins had ever had –
and the noisiest, too.

MORE WALKER PAPERBACKS
For You to Enjoy

The Keeper of the Honey Pot
by Norbert Lande/Hanne Türk

When Susie and Grandpa go off to market, Bruin stays at home to
guard the honey-pot – which turns out to be a very sticky business indeed!
ISBN 0-7445-2081-9 £2.50

Cupboard Bear
by Jez Alborough

Lazy bear just loves to dream
Of his favourite thing – ICE-CREAM!
But bear's sweet dream turns to sour nightmare,
When he finds one day his cupboard's bare!
ISBN 0-7445-1731-1 £2.99

Teddy Tales
by Mirabel and Hugh Cecil

Two lively stories about a household of eighteen bears!
"Clever use of comic strips enhance this witty tale, which should
put the family of bears high on the popularity poll."
ISBN 0-7445-2026-6 *The Surprise Bear*
ISBN 0-7445-2027-4 *The Bears' Christmas*
£2.99 each